# Bunny's Big Balloons

### by Liza Charlesworth

No part of this publication can be reproduced in whole or in part, or stored in a retrieval system, or transmitted in any form or by any means, electronic, mechanical, photocopying, recording, or otherwise, without written permission of the publisher. For permission, write to Scholastic Inc., 557 Broadway, New York, NY 10012.

ISBN: 978-1-338-89041-9

Designer: Cynthia Ng; Illustrated by John Lund

Copyright © 2023 by Liza Charlesworth. All rights reserved. Published by Scholastic Inc.

1 2 3 4 5 6 7 8 9 10   68   31 30 29 28 27 26 25 24 23 22

Printed in Jiaxing, China. First printing, January 2023.

## ▥ SCHOLASTIC

Bunny had fur and floppy ears.
Bird had feathers and a sharp beak.
Bunny liked everything about Bird.
Bird liked everything about Bunny
except for one thing.

What was that one thing?
Bunny NEVER, EVER, EVER shared.
Not a book. Not a toy.
Not even a carrot.

One sunny day, Bunny asked Bird
to go with her to the park.
So off they went.
*Flap, flap, flap!*
*Hop, hop, hop!*

At the park, they rushed to the playground.
They rode on the swings.
They climbed on the jungle gym.
They slid down the slide.
"Wheeeeeee!" they yelled with glee.

Then, they saw the Balloon Raccoon.
He had six big, beautiful balloons—
red, blue, yellow, green, orange, pink!
"Yay!" said Bunny. "I'm glad I have
some money in my purse."

What did Bunny do next?
She bought all six balloons—
red, blue, yellow, green, orange, pink!
Did she give even one to her pal, Bird?
No, Bunny did NOT.

Bunny's selfishness made
Bird VERY mad.
It also made Bunny float
up into the air!

Bunny floated above the grass.
Bunny floated above the jungle gym.
Bunny floated above the slide.
To be honest, she was a little scared.

Bunny floated above the swing set.
Higher and higher she sailed.
To be honest, now she was VERY scared.
How would she get back down to the ground?
"HELP ME!" she cried.

Bird heard Bunny's cry.
"Don't worry, pal!" she shouted.
"I have a plan to save you."
*Flap, flap, flap!*
Bird flew up into the sky.

Bird flew right beside Bunny.
Then, she aimed her sharp beak
at four of the big balloons—
red, blue, yellow, green!
*POP, POP, POP, POP!*

Now Bunny had only two balloons left—
orange and pink.
"HEY, WHY DID YOU DO THAT?"
she yelled with surprise.
"Watch and learn," said Bird calmly.

Bunny DID watch and learn.
It turns out that two balloons was
the perfect number to allow
her to float gently, gently—
back down to the ground.

Bunny landed on a soft patch of grass.
"Thanks," said Bunny. "You are my hero!
I learned an important lesson up there.
From now on, I'll ALWAYS share with my pal."
Then, she gave the big pink balloon to Bird.

"Thank you!" said Bird with a smile.
"Pink is my very favorite color."
After that, Bunny and Bird ran to the slide.
And they slid down it side by side.
"Wheeeeeee!" they yelled with glee.